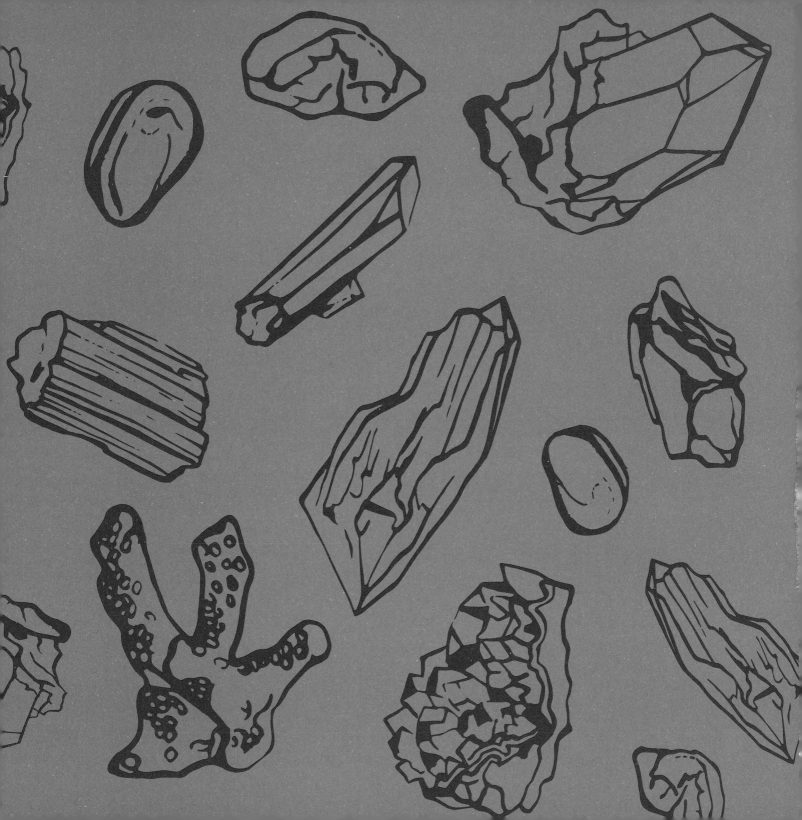

WHERE
WONDER
GROWS

To my mother, Laura, who has never lost her sense of wonder. And to her granddaughters Xarina Yasmin, Xoraya Yxchel, and Yemaya Xol.
—XELENA

To my dad, a gentle soul who taught me to wonder at the details and beauty in all things.
—ADRIANA

WHERE WONDER GROWS

by XELENA GONZÁLEZ

illustrated by ADRIANA M. GARCIA

Cinco Puntos Press
an imprint of Lee & Low Books Inc.
New York

WHEN GRANDMA WALKS TO HER SPECIAL GARDEN,
WE KNOW TO FOLLOW.

THIS IS THE PLACE
WHERE WONDER GROWS
AND STORIES BLOSSOM,

WHERE WE GATHER OUR MAGIC ROCKS
AND RELICS FROM NATURE.

THEY ARE ALIVE WITH WISDOM,
SO WE CALL THEM GRANDFATHERS
AND GRANDMOTHERS.

SHE ASKS US TO WONDER WHY
THIS ONE HAS SO MANY HOLES,
LIKE SECRET ROOMS.

WE LOOK INSIDE TO SEE
MOLTEN HEAT BUBBLING
FROM THE EARTH'S BELLY,
BURNING NEW ROCKS
INTO BEING!

"THEY WERE HERE LONG BEFORE US AND KNOW MORE ABOUT OUR WORLD THAN WE EVER WILL."

GRANDMA SAYS THAT IN THE SWEAT LODGE,
THEY HELP SEND SONGS AND PRAYERS
THROUGH THE AIR, TO OUR ANCESTORS.

"THEY HAVE SURVIVED FIRE,
AND SO THEY GIVE US STRENGTH."

WHEN WE'RE OLD ENOUGH TO ENTER
THE SWEAT LODGE, WE'LL KNOW EXACTLY
WHAT SHE MEANS.

"TELL US ABOUT THE ONES WITH SUPER POWERS," WE ASK.

WE'RE TRANSFIXED BY
THE COLORS OF CRYSTALS
AND THE GLOW OF
GRANDMA'S STORIES...

...ABOUT CURANDERAS WHO CAN CURE THE BODY
WITH WHITE HALITE, SKY BLUE CELESTINE,
AND QUARTZ OF ALL KINDS.

"FROM ITS CORE
TO ITS SURFACE,
OUR EARTH GIVES US
EVERYTHING WE NEED
TO SURVIVE."

AFTER CONJURING FIRE
AND DIGGING DEEP WITHIN EARTH,
IT'S TIME TO DIVE INTO WATER.

WE WONDER WHAT WISDOM
THESE TINY WHITE FORESTS AND
HOUSES OF SHELL HOLD,
DOWN IN THE SEA,
WHERE THERE IS STILL
SO MUCH MYSTERY.

"WATER MAKES AND BREAKS EVEN THE BIGGEST ROCKS,
VERY SLOWLY, OVER TIME."

...SILVER BEAUTIES WHO FLEW
FROM NIGHT'S SKY
LIKE FREED LIGHT
DANCING ON AIR.

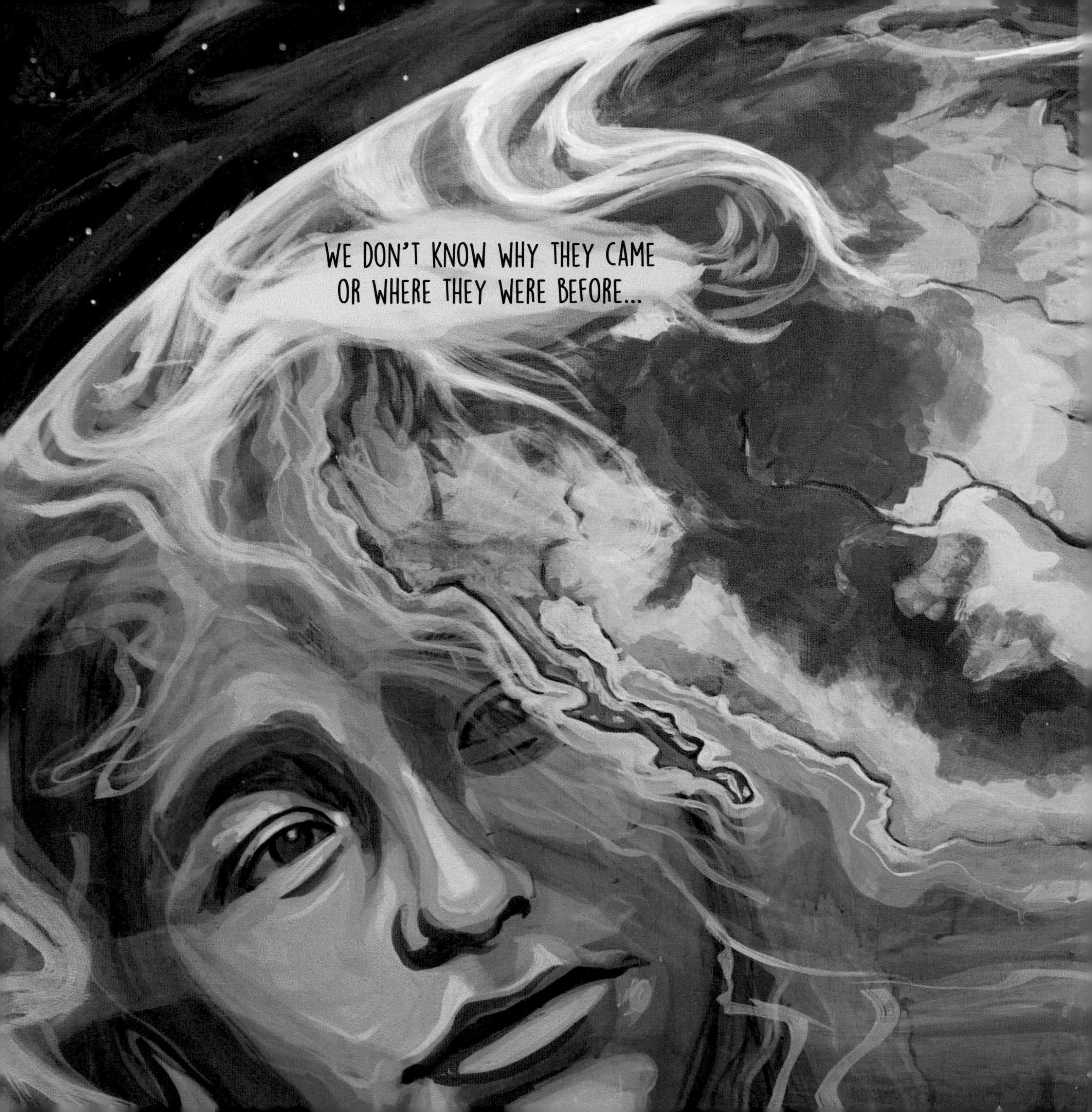
WE DON'T KNOW WHY THEY CAME
OR WHERE THEY WERE BEFORE...

...BUT THERE IS SOMETHING SPECIAL IN THE LAND WE CALL HOME, LIKE MAGNETS THAT DRAW THESE MARVELS FROM OUTER SPACE.

THEY REMIND US
HOW SMALL WE ARE
IN THIS BIG WORLD...
AND HOW VERY POWERFUL.

WHEN THE STARS AWAKEN,
WE REST IN OUR GARDEN,
HOLDING OUR TREASURES CLOSE.

AND WITH EVERY BREATH,
WE CONTINUE TO WONDER.

Dear Reader,

    The idea for this picture book came from you—our readers. Adriana and I have traveled to many schools and libraries around the country. Along the way, you introduced us to your rock finds and friends. You invited us to rock parties, stone painting sessions, and gem hunts. Your belief in the magic of rocks inspired us!

    Adriana and I enjoy making art in unusual ways. She had a strong vision for what this book could be, and I shaped words that would match her splendid paintings. These illustrations are very dear to me because they feature my family (my nieces, my mother, and my daughter—who also appeared alongside my dad in *All Around Us.*)

    We hope that our books remind you of the very special connection you have to your grandparents, your ancestors, and nature. Because of this, you are powerful and enduring. Just like a rock.

Love and light,
Xelena

AUTHOR AND ILLUSTRATOR

    Xelena González (left) and Adriana M. Garcia (right) are the dynamic duo who created *All Around Us*, winner of the Tomás Rivera Mexican American Book Award, a Pura Belpré Illustrator Award Honor, and the American Indian Youth Literature Award Honor, among other accolades. When they are not dreaming up new, unusual books for kids, Xelena stays busy dancing, storytelling, and playing with other writing forms such as scripts, essays, and poems. Adriana can be found painting murals and portraits or designing cool stuff like stage sets and websites. They live and shine in the same Westside neighborhood of San Antonio, Texas, where they were raised.

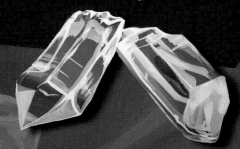

FACTS THAT ROCK

The elements of fire, earth, water, and air are celebrated in various Indigenous ceremonies and art forms. Our book features four relics from nature that represent these four elements: volcanic rocks symbolize fire, crystals represent earth, shells illustrate water, and meteorites express air.

What do you gather in your nature collections? What is their story?

Some people keep their most powerful nature finds in a special place, like Grandma does in her garden. Others carry their treasures with them in a medicine bag. They call it *medicine* because many people can cure and find healing from the stones and plants provided by nature.

Does your family practice any remedios or natural remedies? Where do you carry or keep your special tokens from nature?

A sweat lodge is a ceremonial place where some people go to cleanse their body and spirit by sitting in a natural steam bath, praying and singing alongside people from their Native American community. Various circles practice this custom differently. In our story, the children wait until they're older to enter the lodge, but in some tribes, there are no age limits.

In the Nahuatl language of Mexico, a sweat lodge is called a temazcal. It's fun to say! Can you try it? Do you have any special places where you go to sing or pray with others?

Not all rocks are ready to be collected. Some parks prohibit taking rocks and plants from their natural environment. Before collecting a new find, be sure to check the park rules. And even check with the being itself.

Do you name any of your rock friends? How about shells, trees, or house plants?

Cinco Puntos Press, an imprint of LEE & LOW BOOKS INC., 95 Madison Avenue, New York, NY 10016, leeandlow.com
Designed by Zeke Peña • Production by The Kids at Our House • The text is set in DK Lemon Yellow Sun and Dschoyphul
Manufactured in China by RR Donnelley
First Edition 10 9 8 7 6 5 4 3 2 1
ISBN 9781947627468 (hc) • ISBN 9781947627475 (e-book)
Library of Congress Control Number: 2020943097

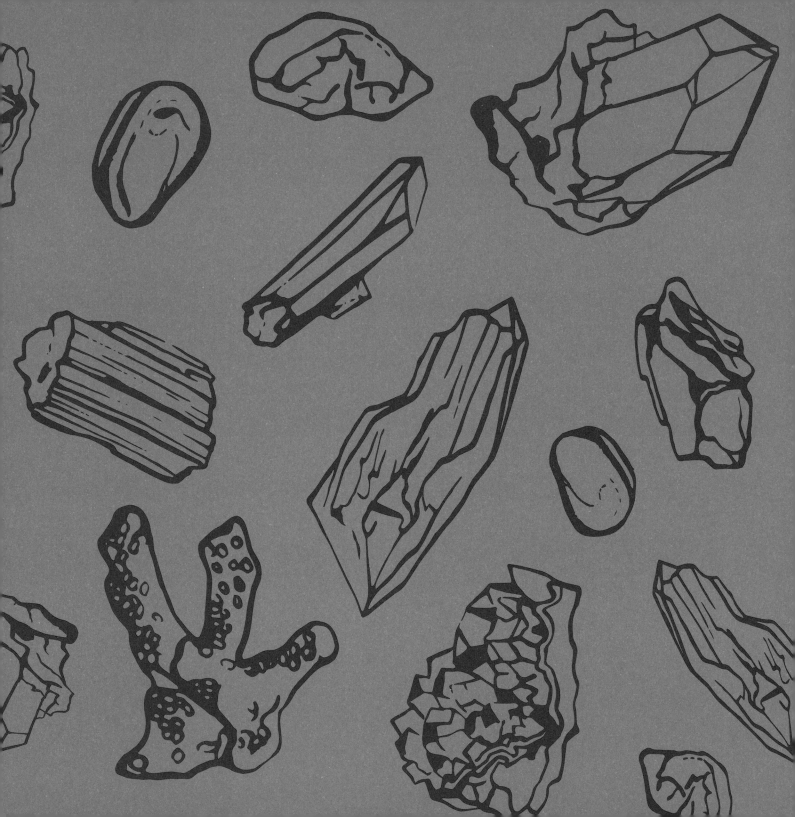